The Strange Museum:
The Royal Switch

Strange Family Home

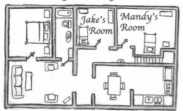

2nd Floor

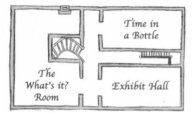

1st Floor

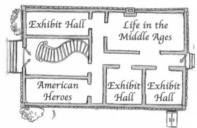

Basement

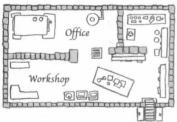

The Strange Museum

STRANGE MUSEUM

The Royal Switch

Written by
Jahnna N. Malcolm

Illustrated by
Sally Wern Comport

Gateway Learning Corporation
2900 S. Harbor Blvd., Suite 202
Santa Ana, CA 92704

ISBN 1-931020-11-6

First Edition
10 9 8 7 6 5 4 3 2 1

To Cleopatra, Queen of Kings
and her sons who are Kings

Contents

Chapter One
The Lost Cat

ere, kitty, kitty!"

Mandy placed a bowl of milk by the back steps to the Strange Museum. She cupped her hands around her mouth and called toward the trash cans at the rear of the parking lot. "Come on, boy. Here's some delicious milk."

Soon two pale gray ears appeared behind one of the cans. Next came a pink nose and a pair of big green eyes. The animal opened its mouth, and Mandy could hear the faintest mew.

"Come on, boy. I won't hurt you. You know

1

that." Mandy sat down on the back stairs and zipped up her navy-blue sweatshirt. There was a definite chill in the air. It felt like snow.

The pale gray cat took several careful steps into the parking lot. He looked over both shoulders and then bolted toward the bowl of milk. The cat was clearly a stray. Mandy could see his ribs poking out from his sides. He seemed a little wobbly on his feet from lack of food.

Mandy placed her hand on his head as the cat lapped up the milk. He started purring instantly. Mandy smiled at the cat.

The cat lifted his head and focused his bright green eyes on Mandy's face. He blinked several times in gratitude, then ducked his head down to finish the rest of the milk.

Mandy continued to pet the cat, brushing his coat with long strokes. The cat arched his back to the touch of her hand. "You like being stroked, don't you," Mandy murmured.

Suddenly the door behind Mandy swung open and her brother, Jake, stuck his head outside. "There you are! Mom was wondering

where you went. We're just about to begin the treasure hunt."

Jake and Mandy worked at the Strange Museum of Lost and Found three days a week after school. On those afternoons, they'd race home, slip into their official guide T-shirts, and prepare to greet the public. Today they were to lead a bunch of school kids on a treasure hunt. The kids were supposed to circle the museum looking for objects from one place in time, like Jolly Old England. Today they were looking for objects from Ancient Egypt.

"Tell Mom I'll be there in a second," Mandy said, trying to block Jake's view of the cat.

At twelve, Jake was two years younger than his sister, but he could read her like a book. "All right, Mandy. What are you hiding?" he asked in a sly voice. "Come on. Let me see."

Mandy stepped aside to show the scrawny gray cat that now sat carefully licking one paw. When he saw Jake, the cat lowered his paw and cocked his head to the right and then to the left, as if he were trying to size him up.

"Well, hello there," Jake said with a grin. He was an animal lover, too.

Of course, as animal lovers go, no one could compare with Mandy. Unlike most of her eighth-grade friends, whose bedroom walls were covered with posters of rock bands and teen stars, Mandy's walls were covered with pictures of cats. There were cat posters, cat calendars, cat birthday cards, and cat drawings on everything. Even her pillows were tiger-striped.

The cat let Mandy pick him up and put him in her lap. "Look at him, Jake. He has the greenest eyes. And even though he's a stray cat, he's so tame. He didn't even flinch when you opened the door."

"He's a really good looking cat," Jake said. "Skinny, but good looking."

"He is good looking, isn't he?" Mandy said. The cat had unusually long, pointed ears and his green eyes were the color of jade.

Jake scratched the cat behind one ear. "How long have you been feeding him?"

"Since the day before yesterday. But he's still

so thin." Mandy pressed her cheek against the top of the cat's head. "Do you think Mom and Dad would let me keep him?"

"No way," Jake replied. "This is a museum. A museum of lost and found *things*. There's no place for a pet."

Mandy's eyes flashed. "Well, this museum is also our home. And we should be able to at least have a cat."

The Strange Museum took up the first two floors of an old mansion. Mandy and Jake lived with their parents on the third floor of the museum.

Mandy hugged the cat close. "It's not like I'm asking for a dog that you have to walk," she complained. "Besides, Mom said once we got the museum going we could talk about getting a pet."

Jake shrugged. "I just know Mom and Dad. They're very picky about this museum's collection. They'd hate to have a cat roaming around scratching and breaking things." Jake leaned forward and whispered in Mandy's ear. "Imagine what might happen to the cat if he got loose in the museum *after* closing time!"

Mandy winced. Jake had a point. Several times she and her brother had found themselves in the Strange Museum after hours. Even though they'd been warned not to touch anything by their parents, they had somehow managed to do just that, which had sent them off on some hair-raising adventures.

When Jake touched a map in the American Heroes display, they were transported back over two-hundred years to Concord. There they joined Paul Revere on his midnight ride.

Mandy's accidental touch of a lantern in their father's workshop had sent them to the shores of North Carolina, where they were captured by Blackbeard the pirate. Jake had knocked a lute off the wall, and they found themselves in the Middle Ages, fighting alongside Robin Hood and his Merry Men.

Mandy could just imagine the problems a cat might cause!

The museum door banged open again, and this time their mother, Kate Strange, stuck her head outside. "What's up with you guys? The treasure hunt is about to start and you two need to lead it."

"Mom, I need to ask you an important question," Mandy said, taking a deep breath.

Mrs. Strange pushed her glasses up on her nose. "I'm sorry, Mandy, but it will have to wait."

"I found this cat—"

"Mandy, there are little kids waiting to start the treasure hunt," her mother interrupted. "We need to get going now!"

"But Mom," Mandy said, holding the cat up for her to see. "This cat needs a home."

There was a loud crash from within the museum and Mrs. Strange called, "We'll have to discuss this later. Hurry, before those kids destroy the museum."

The heavy wooden door closed with a loud thud.

"Sorry," Jake said, patting his sister on the shoulder. "But I told you she'd say no."

After Jake went inside, Mandy sat quietly for several minutes. Then she slowly held the cat up and peered into his big green eyes. "Mom didn't exactly say no. And if you ask me, you're just perfect for our museum. It is a museum of lost and found things. First you were lost—and then I found you!"

Chapter Two
Sneaky Mandy

A few minutes later, Jake and Mandy were leading their two teams of students on the treasure hunt. It covered both floors of the museum.

Each team was given a list of artifacts from Egypt. The kids had to search the museum displays to find each one. The team that located all of its artifacts first was the winner.

Jake's team found its first item right away. It was a bench with legs carved to look like a lion's paws. Then Mandy's team found the first one on its list. It was a wooden model of a boat that sailed the Nile River. It was from an Egyptian tomb.

One of the most valuable artifacts in the museum was a necklace made of three rows of little gold rings. It was called a Hero's Collar.

"Why is it so valuable?" a second grade girl with glasses asked Mandy. "It just looks like a necklace."

"This was a gift from a Pharaoh. The Pharaohs were the kings of Egypt. They gave these gold necklaces as rewards for bravery. Men and women were very proud to wear them." Mandy pronounced the word 'Pharaoh' slowly so the girl could understand it. "The last *fare-oh* ruled over 2,000 years ago," she explained.

The girl's eyes widened. "That necklace is 2,000 years old?" she said in a whisper.

Mandy nodded. "Amazing, isn't it?"

Mandy's group checked off the items on its list: a woman's clip that was handy for hooking cloaks or other garments at the shoulder, and a polished bronze mirror.

Jake's group looked for the carved handle of a

fan. As the kids rushed all over the main floor, Jake called out, "Remember, this isn't just a wimpy little handle. It's a long carved stick."

A few minutes later, one of the boys in his group found a broomstick in the janitor's closet and brought it to Jake.

"Close," Jake said with a chuckle. "But this is used to sweep floors. We're looking for a carved handle of a fan that was used to keep Pharaohs and their queens cool."

Then Jake's group raced upstairs with Jake struggling to keep up with them. They went from room to room, looking in glass cases and on pedestals.

At last a boy shouted, "I found it hanging on the wall!"

"That does it, gang!" Jake told his first- and second-graders. "We've found all of the items on our list. Hurry! We have to run back to the lobby."

His group was running down the stairs as Mandy's group ran from a back room on the main floor. They were all shouting, "We won! We won!" Then they joined together and raced for the lobby.

With all the shouting kids running toward the finish line, Mandy thought she'd be able to sneak away unnoticed.

Jake saw her heading in the direction of the back stairs. He didn't have time to stop her. He had to hurry to catch up with the two teams.

The contest would have been declared a tie, except the little girl with glasses from Mandy's group got to the lobby a few seconds ahead of the others. She was carrying her team's list.

"Here, Mrs. Strange," she said, handing the list to Jake's mom. "I think my team won the treasure hunt."

Mrs. Strange took the list, checked it over, and beamed at the group. "Yes indeed. You've won this hunt, but only by a few seconds. And because of that, you all win a Junior Museum Explorer pass. It's good for one ice cream cone at Scoops Ice Cream Parlor just around the corner."

"Hooray!"

Jake had to cover his ears because the cheering was so loud. He spun in a circle and looked for Mandy. She was nowhere to be seen.

After Mrs. Strange handed out the ice cream passes and said good-bye to the teachers, Jake led the groups to the front door. He waved good-bye and collapsed against the big wooden doors. "I feel like I just ran a marathon."

Mrs. Strange laughed. "It's hard keeping up with first- and second-graders. They're fast." Mrs. Strange did a quick scan of a few of the rooms that surrounded the lobby. "So fast that I think they lost your sister."

"Last I saw of her, she was heading toward the bathroom," Jake said. "She must still be in there."

Mrs. Strange shook her head. "No. I was just there. It's empty."

Jake frowned. "Then Mandy skipped out on me. Boy, is she gonna get it when I find her!"

Mrs. Strange put one hand on his arm. "I'll talk to her later. In the meantime, we received a shipment just before the treasure hunt began. Your father is unpacking it in the basement. I told him I'd help." Mrs. Strange was already heading toward the basement door. "Would you lock up, Jake?"

Jake paused for just a second. "All right."

Locking up was always a little creepy for him. Making sure all of the doors were locked was the easy part. The hard part was turning off the lights and knowing that once he did that, anything could happen. At any time.

Jake had just locked the door to the parking lot out back when he heard a *tap-tap-tap* sound. He went back to the door and listened.

Tap-tap-tap.

There it went again. He unlocked the door and slowly pushed it open. Mandy pushed her face into the opening and whispered, "Is Mom or Dad there?"

Jake shook his head. "They're both in the basement unpacking a new shipment."

"Then let me in quick."

Jake held open the door and Mandy rushed in. Her jacket was wrapped around something in her arms. She carried it very gently, like a baby.

"That had better not be what I think it is," Jake whispered.

"Pretend like you don't even see him," Mandy ordered. "I'm going to keep him in the cloak room. No one ever goes in there. I'll feed him until he gets strong and then find him a home."

Jake locked the back door again and followed his sister down the dark hallway. "Look, when Mom and Dad find that cat, you'd better tell them I had nothing to do with it."

"I promise," Mandy called over her shoulder. She was trying to balance the cat with one arm and turn on the light with the other. Suddenly the cat sprang out of her arms.

Jake watched Mandy's jacket scoot along the floor toward the first room in the museum. Then the cat zipped out from under the jacket into the dark.

"Help me, Jake!" Mandy shrieked. "We've got to catch him before he breaks something."

They heard a loud crash and the sound of glass shattering onto the big marble floors. "Too late," Jake said. "Boy, are you in trouble."

"Oh, like that's helpful." Mandy blew her hair off her face in frustration. "Now come on and help me catch that cat!"

Jake fought the urge to run upstairs and tell

his parents that Mandy's cat had broken something. He knew they would get mad and get rid of the cat. And Jake didn't want to admit it, but he kind of liked the cat.

The two of them hurried on tiptoe into the display room. Jake turned on the light. It wasn't hard to find the cat. They just had to look for the broken glass. It was in the far corner of the room.

"Don't touch a thing!" Mandy warned as they carefully stepped through the pieces of broken glass. "Anything can happen."

"You don't have to tell me," Jake said. "Remember, you're the one who grabbed the lantern that sent us to meet Blackbeard when I told you not to touch it."

He expected Mandy to shoot back some sarcastic remark about him accidentally knocking the lute off the wall, but she didn't say anything. She had stopped dead in her tracks.

"What is it?" He asked joining her.

"Look, the glass is broken, but the cat hasn't run away. He's sitting on the velvet block that holds the Hero's Collar."

Jake and Mandy stood staring at the thin gray cat. He stared right back at them. He didn't seem scared or upset. In fact, he seemed calmer then he had ever looked outside.

"He looks like he belongs there," Jake whispered to Mandy.

"I was just thinking the same thing," Mandy replied. "He acts like the Hero's Collar belongs to him."

"He better not touch it," Jake warned, "or he'll be sent who knows where."

Mandy bit her lip in worry. "I don't know what to do. Should I call him?"

"No," Jake said. "He could accidentally touch the necklace. I think you should just pick up the cat and take him upstairs."

"Upstairs?" Mandy repeated in surprise. "What do you mean?"

"Just grab the cat and go upstairs," Jake said firmly. "Tell Mom and Dad we have to keep this cat, and I'll back you up."

"You will?" Mandy cried. "Jake! You're the best!"

She threw her arms around her brother's neck, which threw him off balance. The two of them tumbled sideways onto the velvet box with the cat and the necklace.

The sound was tremendous. But not of crunching glass, or a cat crying out. It was the enormously loud sound of a wind tunnel as they traveled back, back in time.

Chapter Three
Welcome to Egypt

Though the rushing sound of the wind had stopped, Jake and Mandy still felt a breeze. But it was a warm one. It blew through a graceful archway carved out of stone. They were standing in a room filled with painted pillars.

"Okay, I give up," Jake said. "Where are we?"

"I'm not sure." Mandy was still feeling dizzy from their trip back in time.

They could see a balcony through the open archway. On the balcony was a low bench with cushions. Its legs were carved to look like a lion's paws and looked like the bench from their treasure hunt. A bowl of grapes sat on a small table next to it.

"The cat!" Mandy quickly looked at her feet, where the cat sat calmly looking around them as if nothing had happened. "He came with us."

Draped around the cat's neck was the gold necklace. "And he brought the Hero's Collar with him," Jake cried. "Grab the cat and let's go back."

Mandy bent down to pick up the cat. The sudden movement startled the cat and he bolted through the archway and over the side of the balcony, taking the Hero's Collar with him.

"Oh, great," Jake groaned. "There goes our ticket back to the museum."

Mandy nodded. "That's the bad news."

Jake and Mandy had learned from their other adventures that it was always a lost item from the museum that sent them back in time. When the item was returned to its rightful owner, they could return to their home.

"What's the good news?" Jake asked as they stepped onto the balcony. Beyond the balcony was

a rich garden of tall palm trees and lush flowers.

"I know where we are," Mandy replied, looking over the garden wall at the hundreds of white washed houses that tumbled down to the banks of a great river. The river curved into the distance like a ribbon of gold.

"Are you going to give me a hint?" Jake asked as he reached for a grape in the bowl.

"All right, I will." Mandy pointed at the great river where flat wooden boats with white sails shaped like triangles moved slowly across the water. "That is the Nile River."

Jake nearly choked on his grape. "The Nile? Then this must be Egypt."

"That would be my guess." Mandy stepped to the edge of the balcony to get a better look. "Those boats look a lot like that wooden model we have in the museum."

"Are you sure?" Jake whispered. "Because if you're right, we've gone back over 2,000 years."

Mandy nodded. "The Hero's Collar was from Egypt. The Pharaohs and their queens liked to give them to people as a reward for good deeds," she explained, remembering what she had told her treasure hunt team at the museum.

"So, who are we going to meet this time?" Jake asked, looking around nervously. "Some mummy wrapped in old rags?"

Mandy shivered. "I hope not." She turned in a circle to get a sense of her surroundings. "This doesn't look like any tomb where a mummy would be. It looks like a place where people live, like a house or palace."

Jake ran his hand along the smooth couch. The cushions were covered in a soft violet fabric. "I always thought of Egypt as filled with big stone pyramids and giant statues."

"Me too," Mandy said.

"Look at those paintings on the arch," Jake pointed to the colorful images of lilies and reeds bordering the arch. "They seem almost modern."

Mandy peeked back through the arch into the palace. "And those pillars look like the ones you see in paintings of Greek gods and goddesses."

"I wonder whose palace this is," Jake

whispered, looking around for any sign of people.

As if in answer to his question, Jake heard a girl's voice cry, "It's my home. I'm going to be queen some day. I should be able to do what I want."

The voice was coming their way. Mandy and Jake flattened themselves against the wall on either side of the archway.

A figure swept past them onto the balcony. It was a girl. She had shoulder length black hair with bangs cut straight across her forehead. She wore a dress of pleated white cloth that draped over her shoulders and hung to the floor. All of her jewelry was gold—her necklace, her bracelets, and even the unusual crown that circled her head. It was shaped like a cobra with three heads.

The girl threw herself onto the couch and began to weep.

Jake and Mandy had seen enough pictures and movies to know exactly who she was.

"Cleopatra!" they gasped out loud.

Chapter Four
Princess of the Nile

When Jake and Mandy called her name, Cleopatra didn't look up. She just wailed, "Leave me alone!"

Jake and Mandy's eyes nearly bugged out of their heads. Jake whispered to Mandy, "I can understand her."

Mandy nodded eagerly. "And she can understand us. It's magic."

Jake gestured for Mandy to go to Cleopatra. "Say something else. Just to make sure she knows what we're saying."

"Excuse me, Cleopatra, miss," Mandy said, taking a step toward the girl on the couch. "I just wanted to know why you are crying."

Without looking up, Cleopatra replied, "My life is so boring! I spend all my days with palace guards and servants like you."

Jake raised an eyebrow at his sister but didn't say a word.

"I'm told what to say and think by my father," the dark-haired princess ranted. "I can't do anything I want to do. I have to sit for hours and listen to him *talk*."

Mandy remembered some of the times she had listened to her father go on and on about some piece of art he had found for the museum. It could be very boring. "I know what you mean," she said.

"The only fun I ever have is fighting with my rotten little brother," Cleopatra cried.

Jake perked up at this. "What do you fight about?"

Cleopatra answered as if that was a silly question. "We argue about who will rule Egypt after our father, of course."

Jake and Mandy both knew the answer to that question. It would be Cleopatra, of course. But they decided they had better not tell her.

Cleopatra pounded the couch in anger. "I'm a prisoner in my own home." Then she buried her head in her arms and sobbed. From time to time she made little hiccup sounds.

Jake and Mandy huddled close to each other as they watched Cleopatra cry. They both would have thought the life of a princess was thrilling. It was strange to hear this legend complain that her life was boring. She had no idea how famous she was, or how many books, plays, and even movies, would be made about Cleopatra of Egypt.

"How do you help a bored princess?" Mandy whispered.

"Beats me," Jake said with a shrug. "Fighting with your brother about who gets to rule a whole kingdom sounds pretty exciting to me."

"Me, too," Mandy said. "Maybe we should do something to distract her."

"Hey, why don't we give her a present or

something?" Jake suggested. "That always cheers people up."

Mandy agreed. "Let's see what we've got." She dug in the pockets of her jean skirt and found a pearl-covered barrette and a note that her girlfriend had passed to her in study hall. Jake found some spit wads, a quarter, three gum wrappers and a crumpled stick of gum in his pants.

"Maybe she'd like the gum," he said as he tried to flatten it out. "Or the quarter."

Mandy whispered, "Girls like hair ornaments. No matter what time period they come from." She held up the barrette and walked over to Cleopatra. As she got closer, she cleared her throat to get the girl's attention.

"Cleopatra, um, Your Highness?" Mandy stammered. "I have something that might make you feel better. I put it in my hair. You might like to wear it in yours."

The mention of a present made Cleopatra stop crying. She raised her head to look at Mandy.

"Whoa!" Jake yelped as he saw the princess's

face for the first time. "It's like double vision!"

Both girls spun to look at Jake. "What?"

Cleopatra wore very thick black eye liner with green eye shadow, and she had bangs. But other than that, she looked exactly like Mandy.

"You could be twins!" Jake gasped.

Chapter Five
Twins!

Mandy had always wondered what it would be like to have a twin. But this was too weird for words. She stood frozen in place, staring at Cleopatra's face.

Cleopatra did the same. She opened and closed her mouth several times before she spoke. Finally she gasped, "How is this possible? Who are you?"

Mandy was still too shocked to speak, so Jake took over. He bowed at the waist just like he'd seen some actors do in a movie about Roman gladiators.

He also tried to speak in a formal way. "I know this may sound strange, oh great Queen-to-Be, but my sister and I have come from another country and another time."

Jake's words brought Mandy back. She tried to stop him from telling the truth. She was sure Cleopatra wouldn't believe it. But Jake held up a hand, warning his sister not to speak.

"We have been sent by the gods to help you with your problem," he continued.

Mandy flinched. She was sure Cleopatra would get mad at what Jake was saying, but she didn't. Instead Cleopatra said, "Which gods?"

Jake looked quickly around him. Everywhere he looked—on the floor, on the pillars—the name "Isis" was written beneath paintings and sculptures of a female goddess. In all of the paintings other Egyptians were kneeling or bowing in front of the goddess.

"We come from the goddess Isis," he said, hoping he had pronounced it correctly. He said "*Eye-sis.*"

Cleopatra seemed pleased to hear this. "Go

on. I am ready to hear your words."

Jake gulped. "You see, we know what it is to fight with a brother or sister over who is most powerful. We also know what it is like to have a father who can be a total bore. And sometimes, when we have been grounded, we too have known what it is like to be a prisoner in our own home."

Mandy rolled her eyes. Jake was really pushing it.

But Cleopatra seemed to believe every word Jake said. "What does the goddess Isis say that I should do?" she asked.

Jake scratched his head. "She thinks you should have a party and invite some of your friends."

"The goddess suggests this?" Cleopatra frowned. "But I am a princess. I have no friends."

"What? No friends!" Jake repeated. "Then you should go out and get some before it's too late."

Mandy jabbed her brother with her elbow to let him know that she was taking over. "I think what this messenger is saying, Your Highness, is that you should maybe get involved in some activities with other girls your age. Like, take up a sport. There must be some clubs you could join."

"Clubs?" Jake stomped on his sister's foot.

"Ow!" Mandy caught her foot in one hand and hopped around in a circle. "Why did you do that?" she hissed at her brother.

Jake pulled her over to the side of the balcony. "What kind of clubs do you think they have here in Egypt?" Jake whispered. "The Let's Make a Mummy Club?"

Mandy blushed. Her brother was right. They probably didn't have teen clubs 2,000 years ago. At least not the kind she knew about.

"You're going to blow our messenger cover," Jake continued. "And I've seen enough movies to know we could be demoted to the level of slave in the blink of an eye."

Mandy gulped. "Okay, I'm sorry. I'll try to be more careful."

They went back to Cleopatra, who was too wrapped up in her own misery to notice their argument.

"You should go out among your people,"

Mandy suggested. "Get to know them. See how they live and make friends with them." She tried to use her best messenger-from-the-goddess-Isis voice.

Cleopatra's eyes widened. "I would love that!" She sat up and smiled. "It would be wonderful to be a normal girl. Even if it was only for one day."

Jake shrugged. "Then, in the words of the goddess Nike, who was fond of footwear, just do it."

Cleopatra stood up and said, "I will. I'll dress as a peasant girl." She pointed to Mandy's jeans and sweatshirt. "Like you."

It was hard for Mandy not to feel a little insulted about her clothes. But she forced a big smile and said, "Good idea."

Cleopatra paced in a circle around the balcony. "Let's see. What do I have to do today? I have my Latin lesson with my tutor."

"Latin?" Mandy said. "I thought we were in Egypt. Why would you need to know Latin?"

Cleopatra narrowed her eyes. "I am fluent in many languages. But Latin is the speech of Rome, and Rome is the most powerful nation in the world. My father says *everyone* should know Latin."

"Geez," muttered Jake. "Her dad sounds just like Mrs. Waxman, our French teacher."

"But I can cancel that lesson," Cleopatra declared. "Kali!" She clapped her hands twice and called out, "Kali! Come here."

Instantly a serving girl appeared in the archway. The girl dropped to her knees and bent forward, pressing her forehead to the ground. "I await your command, oh Princess."

"I am going to leave the palace for a short time," Cleopatra announced. She pointed to Mandy. "This stranger has been sent by the goddess Isis to make this happen. Obey her as you would me."

The girl named Kali just nodded her head.

"See to it that this goddess gets everything she wants," Cleopatra went on.

"Yes, oh Princess," Kali replied.

"Oh, and tell my tutor that I won't be taking my Latin lesson today," Cleopatra added. "Tell him I am ill and have gone to my room to rest."

"Yes, oh Princess," Kali said, her head

bobbing up and down as she spoke. She began to back out of the room.

"And tell any who comes to my door that I am seeing no one today," Cleopatra added. "Let no one enter. That is my wish and my command."

Kali bowed again and was gone.

Cleopatra looked back at Jake and Mandy. "See? It's done."

"What is done?" Mandy asked.

Cleopatra shrugged. "You will take my place while I am gone."

"Now just a minute!" Mandy protested. "This is insane. I can't take your place. No one would ever believe it. And besides—"

Cleopatra held up her hand for silence, and Mandy stopped talking. "The goddess Isis has given you my features to make my trip among my people possible." Cleopatra looked at Jake. "Correct?"

Jake didn't know what else to say, so he answered, "Correct."

Cleopatra looked at Mandy and smiled. "Then it must be so."

If Mandy could have punched her brother, she would have. Instead she said, "Well . . . I suppose I could sit in your room while you went out for an hour or two. Just as long as no one came in."

"Don't worry, no one will come in," Cleopatra said lightly. "You are ill, remember?"

Cleopatra had already left the balcony and was walking through the room with the painted pillars. She didn't look behind to see if Jake and Mandy were following. They hurried after her into another room. The stone floor was covered in rich carpets. Several carved wooden chairs like the one they'd seen on the balcony were placed around the room.

There were servants everywhere they turned. Two young women knelt by a tiled pool full of water. The girl called Kali and several others knelt on either side of a low table filled with bowls of food. When they saw Cleopatra, they bowed and waited for the young princess to give them an order.

"I thought you said there would be nobody

here," Mandy whispered out of the corner of her mouth. "Who are these people?"

"Them?" Cleopatra said with a wave of the hand. "They're just servants. You don't have to worry about them."

"See?" Jake nudged his sister with his elbow. "It will be easy."

Mandy glared at her brother, who was standing beside her with a smug grin on his face. She pointed to his jeans and T-shirt. "And how do I explain *him*?" she asked Cleopatra.

Cleopatra grabbed a large carved pole with a fan of ostrich feathers at one end. It looked just like the fan that had been in the museum's treasure hunt. She handed it to Jake. "For today, you will be the Royal Fan Bearer."

Jake looked disappointed. "Thanks a lot."

Cleopatra blinked at him in surprise. "It is a great honor. Many fan bearers have their own tombs."

Now it was Mandy's turn to nudge Jake. "See? If you play your cards right, you could get your own tomb."

Jake forced a smile. "I can't wait."

"You stay here," Cleopatra told Jake as she pulled Mandy behind a large curtain. "Make sure no one steps one foot beyond this curtain."

"And keep a lookout for that green-eyed cat," Mandy whispered. "Remember, he's our way home."

"Wait a minute!" All at once Jake felt weird being the only guy in a room full of girls. "What are you two going to do?"

Cleopatra gave him a sly smile. "We are going to trade places."

Chapter Six
Trading Places

Cleopatra's dressing room was almost as big as the other rooms. A little fountain sat at one end, and water trickled from it into a pool surrounded with plants. At the other end an arched door led into the palace gardens. The smell of cinnamon filled the air.

Cleopatra's dresser was covered with painted pots and glass jars. There were several carved figures of girls holding bowls in their arms. Each bowl was filled with a different colored powder.

There were live animals, too. Bamboo cages

full of songbirds sat on marble stands or hung on hooks from pillars. Some tiny monkeys played together in a far corner. But there was not a single cat.

Cleopatra removed her gold crown with the three cobra heads. "Normally one of my maids helps me get ready for any outings," she explained as she set the crown on the dressing table. "But this will have to be our secret."

Mandy had a terrible sinking feeling in the pit of her stomach. "I have given this a great deal of thought, Princess," Mandy declared. She tried to make her voice sound strong, but it had a funny little wobble in it anyway. "And I am not sure that trading places is such a good idea."

Cleopatra slapped Mandy on the back and laughed. "That is very funny, since you are the one who thought of it. Now please, sit in the chair, messenger from Isis, and I will complete your transformation into me."

Mandy sank down onto the chair in front of the dresser. She tried to think of some way to talk Cleopatra out of making the switch, but nothing came to mind.

Meanwhile, Cleopatra opened her little jars of makeup and got to work.

"First we have to do something about your eyes," she said. "You may be a messenger from the goddess, but just between you and me, you certainly don't look very goddess-like."

She dipped a tiny brush into a pot of something wet and black and outlined Mandy's eyes with it. With another brush she shaded Mandy's eyes in a deep green color.

"This is my favorite," Cleopatra confided. "It comes from a little town on the Red Sea, and I have to send a special messenger for some every month."

She used a piece of sponge to dab some orange and red powder on Mandy's cheeks and lips.

"There. That should do it." Cleopatra held up a mirror for Mandy to see her new self. The mirror was just a thin circle of metal that had been polished to a fine gloss, like the one in the treasure hunt.

Mandy gasped as she saw her reflection. "That's *me*?"

"No," Cleopatra said with her sly smile. "That is *me*." The princess looked down at Mandy's clothes and shook her head. "Almost. Those clothes will never do."

She opened one of the big leather trunks lining the walls and pulled out a long white silk dress. "Put this on, and give me your clothes."

Mandy knew if they were going to successfully trade places, she had better do as she was told.

While Mandy dressed up as the princess, Cleopatra was busy putting on her own disguise. She pulled a short cotton dress out of a trunk and slipped it over her head. There were a few small holes near the hem, which Cleopatra tore open to make the dress look even more ragged than it was. Then she tied a piece of cotton cord around her waist as a belt.

Next she took a large sponge, dipped it in water, and wiped all the makeup off her face. Cleopatra took off all of her rings and bracelets and dropped them into a wooden box on the table. Mandy tried not to stare. The rings were studded with jewels and must have been worth a fortune.

Finally the two girls faced each other.

Mandy could not believe her eyes. Cleopatra really looked like her, and she really looked like the famous princess. "I don't believe it."

Cleopatra shook her head. "There's something missing." She stared at Mandy for a few seconds, then snapped her fingers. "Of course! I almost forgot it."

"What?" Mandy asked.

Cleopatra tugged at the hair on top of her own head and it came off. She was wearing a wig! Underneath the wig, her own hair was pulled into a bun at her neck.

"This." Cleopatra set the dark black wig on Mandy's head. "*Now* you are Cleopatra." She looked down at her own simple clothes and giggled with mischief. "And I am a perfect nobody. How wonderful!"

With that she turned and skipped through the arched door into the garden.

"Wait a minute!" Mandy called after her.

"Don't you have anything you want to tell me?"

Cleopatra stopped and turned. "Hmm.... Let me think." She rubbed her chin with her hand. "Don't let Tolly see you."

Mandy shook her head. "Tolly? I don't understand."

Cleopatra giggled. "I'm sorry. I mean, my brother the prince. His name is Ptolemy, but I

call him Tolly just to irritate him." She scowled. "I hate him and, of course, he despises me and will do anything to see that I don't become queen. Don't talk to him, and all will be well."

She turned and ran into the garden.

"Is that all?" Mandy called after her.

"Oh, and whatever you do, stay away from Ash," Cleopatra called over her shoulder.

Mandy ran after Cleopatra into the garden and shouted, "Who is Ash?"

But Cleopatra had already vanished into the maze of bushes. All Mandy could hear was a faint, "I'll be back before dark!"

Chapter Seven
Walk like an Egyptian

Pssst!" Mandy whispered from behind a silk curtain. "Jake!"

Jake didn't seem to hear her. He had wrapped himself in a sheet of gold fabric and was chatting with the royal pool girls.

"Hey!" Mandy shouted. "Royal Fan Bearer! Get over here!"

When Jake turned and saw his sister, he didn't recognize her at first. He bent at the waist and said, "What can I do for you, oh Queen-to-Be?"

Mandy inched into the room and whispered

out of the corner of her mouth, "It's me, Jake. The future queen has split the scene."

Jake's eyes nearly bugged out of his head. "Mandy! I can't believe it's you. You look so, so—"

"Beautiful?" Mandy finished for him.

Jake shook his head. "No. I was going to say old."

"Yeah," Mandy joked. "Like 2,000 years old."

They would have laughed but a man stepped into the room and announced, "The great Ash, advisor to His Highness the Pharaoh, requests an audience with Egypt's princess."

"The great Ash!" Mandy turned to Jake in a panic. "Cleopatra said to keep away from him. Don't let him in. Tell him I'm sick."

"What?" Jake croaked as Mandy raced back into the dressing room.

Jake turned as a large man entered the room. He was wearing a wrap of short white cloth around his waist, and a big gold and blue necklace that looked like a collar. On his head was a cone-shaped hat. Jake would have laughed except for the hard expression on the man's face.

"Who are you?" the great Ash demanded.

From the way the man acted, Jake knew that he had the power to turn Jake from a Royal Fan Bearer into a slave with just a snap of his fingers.

Jake held up the ostrich feather fan with one hand and bowed his head. "I am the new Royal Fan Bearer."

The great Ash raised an eyebrow. "What has happened to the old one?"

"He, um, called in sick," Jake said, "so the princess asked me to fill in for him today."

"Called in sick?" the man repeated.

Jake suddenly remembered that they didn't have phones in old Egypt so he quickly added, "He sent a messenger."

The man frowned and looked around. "Where is the princess?"

"I think she caught a cold from her fan bearer. And now she's sick."

"She can't be," the man said.

"What do you mean?"

"The prince of Persia wishes to meet her. He's traveled for many days. She knows how important this visit is to her father, and to Egypt."

"She does?" Jake asked. He knew his sister was on the other side of the screen, hanging on every word. "I'll see if she is feeling any better."

"Tell her I won't have any of her childish nonsense," the man snapped. "Not today. The banquet is ready. She must appear in the Hall of Feasts *now*!"

"I will tell her, oh Great One," Jake said, bowing at the waist. He kept bowing and backed all the way back around the silk drape where Mandy was hiding.

"Bad news," Jake whispered.

"I heard," she said. "What do we do?"

"The only thing we can do," Jake said. "Run!"

"Good idea!" Mandy said, "You lead the way."

Jake stepped out from behind the screen and instantly popped back in. "More bad news. There are twenty girls waiting to help you get ready for the banquet with the prince of Persia."

Mandy had already started to remove her Cleopatra disguise. She paused with the crown in midair. "Then we'll have to go to Plan B."

"Plan B?" Jake asked. "I don't remember that plan. Give me a hint."

"We make a run for it, but we take the royal escorts with us," Mandy said as she put the crown back on her head. "We'll let the girls lead us through the palace toward the banquet. But instead of stopping at the banquet, we'll keep going through the gardens and out of this palace."

Jake wasn't exactly convinced that this was a good plan, but he didn't have any better ideas. He shrugged. "Whatever you say, oh Queen-to-Be."

Jake stepped out from behind the curtain. Kali and the other girls were waiting to receive their orders. He clapped his hands twice. "Her Royal Highness would like to take a walk before the banquet. She would be pleased to have all of you join her."

Apparently the servants weren't used to leaving Cleopatra's quarters. There was quite a lot of scurrying around as they checked each other's hair and clothes. When they were ready to go, Jake gave another set of instructions. "Be on the lookout for a gray cat."

"Cat?" Kali repeated. "But there are many gray cats. They are the Pharaoh's sacred cats."

"This one is very special," Jake explained. "He has green eyes and is wearing a gold collar."

There were more murmurs of excitement as the servants prepared for their mission.

Then Jake added, "The one who finds the cat will receive a treasured gift from the Pharaoh's daughter."

Jake stuck his head back inside the dressing room and whispered, "All right, the gang is ready for the big cat hunt."

"Cat hunt?" Mandy hadn't been listening. She was piling on every piece of Cleopatra's jewelry she could find. She wanted to look as regal as she could, in case they ran into any representatives from the prince of Persia.

Jake grabbed his fan. "I'll explain on the way."

Jake and Mandy slipped out of Cleopatra's quarters and headed down the hall. Twenty servants trailed behind them

Mandy looked behind her and grinned. "We look like a parade."

Jake twirled his fan like a baton and aimed it in front of him. He pointed toward a gigantic hall of pillars. At one end he could see green gardens, palm trees, and a high white wall. "This way, oh Great One."

They made a funny sight as the group moved over the painted floors. They wove in and out of the brightly decorated pillars. As they went, all twenty girls looked behind potted trees and around the edges of indoor pools for the gray cat. All of them wanted to win the treasured gift from Cleopatra.

"Sure hope they find that cat," Jake whispered as they crossed an open courtyard that had an extra large fountain at its center.

"But once we find the cat, we still have to find the owner of the necklace and give it back to him or her," Mandy whispered back. "That's the only way we'll be able to get home."

"Right. Now, let's pick up the pace," Jake murmured. "Before someone sees us."

As if in response to his words, a boy's voice called out from behind them.

"Where do you think you're going, Cleo?"

Mandy spun around. A boy about twelve years old stood behind them, dressed in a short white robe and gold sandals. His arms were crossed and he looked impatient. On his head he wore a crown. It was just like Cleopatra's—a gold band with three cobra heads.

There was no doubt in Mandy's mind who this was. She gulped and said, "Tolly! my, uh—brother. What a surprise."

Chapter Eight
Oh, Brother!

The young man put a hand on his hip. "I asked you a simple question. Where are you going?" His tone of voice was very snotty.

Mandy put her hand on her hip and matched his tone of voice. "That's none of your business."

Jake was shocked to hear his sister speak that way to Cleopatra's brother. He hit her on the head with his fan and whispered, "What are you doing? How can you talk to a prince like that?"

"He's my brother," Mandy said between

clenched teeth. "I mean, *her* brother, remember? We fight all the time. Now back off, Royal Fan Bearer!"

Jake bowed and stayed in that position. "Sorry, oh Queen-to-Be. You're right. As usual."

Cleopatra's brother strolled down the hall toward Mandy and Jake. He spoke in a sickeningly sweet voice. "Trying to skip out on the prince of Persia?"

"Of course not," Mandy shot back. "I was on my way to greet the prince right now."

"Oh really." Tolly gestured with his thumb behind him. "The prince is that way, in the Hall of Feasts." He smirked and added, "The room you just passed."

"I knew that," Mandy said, hoping he didn't see her face turning red. Then she added, "I was just getting a small gift to present to him."

She stepped through the nearest arch into the garden. Looking around, she saw a white lotus flower in full bloom floating in the pond. She plucked it from the water and held it up for Cleopatra's brother to see. "And here it is."

Tolly scowled in response.

Mandy turned regally and marched in the direction the young prince had pointed. " You can wait in your room," she called over her shoulder. "Or you can join us. I don't really care."

"You should," Tolly called. "Father is planning to marry you off to the prince of Persia. And you know what that means. When Father dies, I will become the next Pharaoh."

Mandy stopped dead in her tracks. Cleopatra hadn't mentioned anything about this. Mandy wondered if she even knew about it.

"That's not true," Mandy said without turning around.

"Is too," Tolly replied. "I overheard Father telling his plan to Ash. Your marriage to the prince will seal our treaty of friendship with the Persians. Father said he was keeping it a secret from you."

Mandy spun to look at Cleopatra's brother. "But why would he keep it a secret?"

"He knows you'd try to find a way to weasel out of it."

Mandy opened and closed her mouth but didn't know what to say.

Cleopatra's brother crowed with laughter. "Ha-ha! I've beaten you at last." Then he turned and actually skipped off down the hall. He was still laughing when he disappeared around the corner.

Mandy turned to Jake. "Who would have thought brothers could be as big a jerk 2,000 years ago as they are today."

"Hey!" Jake protested. "I never act like that."

Mandy shot him a look that said, "Oh, really?" and Jake added quickly, "Well, maybe sometimes. But I would never be happy about you having to marry some old fat guy with a beard."

"Who said the prince of Persia was old and fat?" Mandy asked.

"I did," Jake replied. He pointed behind Mandy. "Isn't that him?"

They had come to the entrance of the Hall of Feasts. Servants hurried around bringing huge platters of food to the long tables, which were already piled high with steaming dishes. Along each table was a row of low couches, each with a raised cushion at one end.

A large man with a bushy gray beard and a great round belly lay on one of the couches, eating grapes. He snapped his fingers, and a servant raced to fill his drinking cup.

Mandy ducked behind a pillar before the man could see her. All twenty of her serving girls lined up behind the pillar with her.

"That's the prince of Persia?" Mandy gasped. "He's so big he has to lie down to eat!"

Jake peeked his head around the pillar and said, "I think that's the way they eat here."

"How do you know?" Mandy asked.

"It's in our museum," Jake told her. "We have drawings of it. The people of Cleopatra's time would lie down on couches to eat. They'd lean on their left arm and eat with their right hand."

Mandy made a face. "Weird."

They watched the man shovel food into his mouth and shout at the servants in a loud booming voice. Bits of food hung from his beard. He wiped his sticky fingers on his robe and grabbed another bunch of grapes.

"No way is that guy going to marry Cleopatra," Mandy said firmly.

"Who's going to stop him?" Jake asked.

Mandy straightened the crown on top of her black wig. She set her chin in a regal pose and stepped out from behind the pillar.

"Me."

Chapter Nine
The Prince of Persia

Mandy had a plan. She would make the prince of Persia despise her. By the end of the dinner he would be on his knees begging her not to marry him. Mandy stepped away from the pillar and gestured for Cleopatra's handmaid, Kali, to join her.

Kali came forward and bowed. "What is it you wish, My Princess?"

"I want to meet the prince of Persia," Mandy whispered. "Would you announce me?"

Kali stayed bent at the waist but tilted her head so Mandy could hear her whisper, "That is the job of the Royal Fan Bearer." Then Kali stood up and spoke directly to Jake. "Remember, My Princess is *always* called Cleopatra, the Sun God's daughter."

Jake nodded. "Thanks, Kali," he said with a twirl of his fan. "I can take it from here."

Waving his fan in the air like a flag, Jake led Mandy, Kali, and the twenty serving girls into the Hall of Feasts. They waited at the door as he marched to the center of the room.

"Ladies and gentlemen, princes and kings," Jake announced. "I come before you to stand behind you, to introduce a lady who needs no introduction. In her life she will be called the Queen of the Nile and the Queen of Kings, but everyone knows her as the Sun God's daughter."

Jake turned to look at Mandy, who gave him a tiny thumbs-up sign. Then he boomed in his loudest voice, "So let's give it up for Cleopatra, the once and future queen!"

At first the guests at the banquet were

stunned by this strange announcement. They didn't know what to do or say. Then Jake began to clap his hands. He marched from table to table getting the guests to clap. Then he started to chant, "Cleo! Cleo!"

The guests grinned and began to clap and chant with Jake. Soon the whole room was cheering. That's when the twenty serving girls danced into the room, throwing rose petals as they came. That was Kali's idea. Then Mandy made her grand entrance. She walked through the pile of rose petals, her head held high.

"Don't look to the left or to the right," Kali had told her. "Walk slowly. The world will wait for Cleopatra."

Mandy paraded down the center of the Hall of Feasts like a bride heading for the altar. When she reached the prince of Persia, he had gotten up off the couch and was waiting for her. She extended her hand, and he bent to kiss it. But Jake slammed the ostrich feather fan down on her hand, and the prince of Persia got a mouth full of feathers.

He started choking, and Jake slapped him on the back. "Sorry about that, big guy, but Princess Cleopatra doesn't like to be kissed."

Mandy winked at Jake, then said, "The Sun God's daughter welcomes the Prince of Persia to her country. Are you enjoying our food?" Before the prince could answer, Mandy surprised everyone by patting his round stomach and saying, "Well, I guess so. What do you think, oh Royal Fan Bearer?"

Jake peered at the prince's belly. "Whoa there, your hugeness. You are about to win the Porky Prince Award."

Mandy pulled the prince's plate away from him. "We're cutting you off. Sorry." She snapped her fingers. "Tell the royal chef that from now on this guy only gets carrot sticks and cottage cheese. And no dessert."

At first the prince thought she was flirting with him, but then he realized she was making fun of him. He lowered his voice and directed his question only at Mandy. "Do you mock the prince of Persia?"

Mandy met his gaze. "I don't mock you," she said. "I mock a marriage with you."

This brought gasps from some of the tables, and even from the servants. The hall was so quiet you could hear a pin drop. That was how Jake and Mandy heard the tiny *meow* that came from under the prince's table.

Jake ducked down to look under the table. "Mandy!" he cried. "It's that cat. And he's still wearing the gold necklace."

Mandy completely forgot that she was supposed to be Cleopatra and dropped to her knees. "Here, kitty, kitty!" she called.

The cat blinked his big green eyes at her. Mandy felt the cat's soft fur rub against her hand. "Good boy," Mandy whispered as her fingers closed around the collar.

Just then the prince of Persia popped his head under the table. "What is going on here?" he demanded.

His booming voice so frightened the cat that it hissed and ran. Mandy tried to hang on by the Hero's Collar, but she couldn't. Quick as a wink the cat darted out from under the table.

Mandy scowled at the prince. "You scared him," she snapped. " Now we'll never get home!"

"Home?" the prince repeated. "What are you talking about?"

Mandy ignored him and shouted to Jake and her servants, "Grab that cat! Jump on him. Do anything you can to catch him."

Mandy expected the servants to obey instantly, just like they always did. But nobody moved. They looked at Kali nervously.

"That cat is sacred to us," Kali explained. "We would never jump on it."

Mandy raised her head to speak to them and bumped it against the table. Her wig and crowned were knocked sideways. When she stood up, her own hair fell out of the wig to her shoulders. The whole room gasped.

"What?" Mandy turned to Jake. "What are they staring at?"

It was the prince of Persia who replied, not Jake.

"Imposter!" he shouted, pointing at Mandy.

"She cannot be Cleopatra."

Mandy quickly straightened the wig. She turned to Kali and asked, "Is he saying that because my wig fell off?"

Kali shook her head. "He says that because you told us to jump on the cat."

Mandy could feel little beads of sweat form on her forehead. "But that was just an expression—a way of speaking." An urgent tone came into her voice. "I mean, I *love* cats. Especially that one. I want to keep him for my pet."

But no one was listening to her. The room was in an uproar as Cleopatra's brother and the captain of the guards ran into the room.

"Send for my father the Pharaoh," Cleopatra's brother shouted. "He will settle this at once."

Mandy whispered out of the side of her mouth, "That is the one person we do NOT want to meet."

"My thoughts exactly," Jake replied. "So what should we do?"

Mandy shrugged. "What we always do—run!"

Mandy threw her lotus flower at the prince of Persia's face, then leaped on top of the table and over the back of his couch. She ran as fast as she could for the nearest door. Jake followed at full speed, swinging his fan at anyone who got too close.

There was such confusion in the room that they were able to run out into the garden. It was dotted with round pools of light from the glowing lanterns that hung from the pillars.

One of Cleopatra's serving girls was waiting for them in the garden. "I have found your cat, My Princess!"

She bowed her head and held out the gray cat, which was still wearing the Hero's Collar. Mandy scooped it up in her arms and gushed, "Thank you, thank you. You've saved our lives."

The girl stayed with her head bowed and her hands outstretched. "I am ready, My Princess."

"For what?" Mandy asked, looking nervously behind her.

"My treasured gift," the girl replied, reminding them of the promise of a reward for the person who found the cat.

"Jake!" Mandy shrieked. "Give her the treasured gift!"

Jake stared at her wide-eyed for a moment. Then he said, "Oh! The treasured gift. Right."

He pulled off his gold toga and dug in the pocket of his pants. He pulled out a quarter, two gum wrappers, and a stick of gum. "Here is your reward," Jake announced, pressing the stuff into the girl's hands. "You earned it."

Mandy wrapped the cat in Jake's gold toga material and shouted, "Now, let's get out of here!"

They hurried out to the big white wall that separated the garden from the city beyond.

Night was falling, and the first stars had appeared in the sky. Behind them lay the palace and certain doom. In front of them was the maze of the city. There was no question which way they should go.

Jake and Mandy, still holding the cat, leaped over the wall into the darkness below.

Chapter Ten
Find Cleopatra!

When Mandy and Jake jumped off the wall surrounding the palace, they expected to land on bushes or rocks. They did not expect to land on a person.

"Ow!" a voice shrieked. "Get off me!"

"Sorry!" Mandy, who was still holding the cat, tried to untangle herself from the stranger beneath her. Jake's fan was jammed in a nearby bush and had pinned him on top of the person, so he couldn't get up at all.

"If you don't get off of me this minute," the

person threatened Jake, "I'll have your head."

Jake twisted the fan back and forth until it finally came free from the bush. He jumped to his feet and held the long pole in front of him like a lance. "Just try it!" he growled, hoping he sounded tough.

Mandy positioned herself behind her brother and guarded the cat. The person they had knocked down slowly stood up. A piece of cloth covered his head so they couldn't see his face.

"Fools," the stranger warned in a muffled voice. "You have no idea who you are threatening."

"And you have no idea who I am," Jake shot back. He aimed a couple of karate kicks into the air, and made a few "Hi-yah!" cries to go with them.

The stranger didn't move. Mandy was impressed. Even though she thought Jake looked kind of silly waving a feather fan and kicking into the air, most people would have shown some worry when faced with an obviously crazy person. But the stranger didn't even flinch.

"Jake, quit it!" Mandy ordered her brother to

stop. "You look like an idiot."

"Jake?" The stranger's voice jumped to a higher tone. "Messenger from Isis?"

Jake stopped kicking and lowered his fan. "Cleopatra?"

Cleopatra took the scarf off her head. "Yes, it's me." She frowned. "But what are you doing here? You were supposed to stay in my room."

"And you were supposed to be back before dark," Mandy called from behind Jake.

Before the two girls could get into an argument, Jake explained, "We were worried about your delay. We thought we had better come find you. Are you all right?"

Now Cleopatra's frown turned into a bright smile. "I'm more than all right. I'm wonderful! I have had the time of my life."

Mandy looked nervously back at the wall behind them. Any second the guards could appear. She tried to warn Cleopatra of the pending problem, but the princess was too excited about her recent adventure to listen.

"I walked the streets and talked to all sorts of

people," Cleopatra continued. "Then I discovered a new game. I call it Knock and Run."

Jake cocked his head. "Okay, I give up. What's Knock and Run?"

Cleopatra's eyes sparkled in the moonlight. "First, you look for a home that has people inside eating or working. Then you knock on the door very loudly and run."

Jake looked guiltily over his shoulder at Mandy. He had done that a couple of times with his friends, but he didn't like to admit it.

"I loved it," Cleopatra clapped her hands together. "And I am going to play it again soon."

Mandy was finally able to cut into the conversation. "You'll have to find someone else to stand in for you," she said. "Our time here is up."

Cleopatra frowned. "You're not leaving, are you?"

"We have to," Jake looked up at the white wall shining in the moonlight above them. "But if I were you, I wouldn't go back to the palace right now. Dinner was a disaster."

"Dinner?" Cleopatra looked sharply at

Mandy. "You were supposed to stay in my room."

"I would have," Mandy explained, "but the prince of Persia showed up."

"The Prince of Persia!" Cleopatra repeated. "He wasn't supposed to come until tomorrow."

"Well, he came today. And he is one angry guy," Jake said. "He's called for your father, the Pharaoh."

Cleopatra's face went pale in the moonlight. All at once she looked like a very scared young girl. "This is not good news. I must return to the palace immediately." She scrambled up the rocky hillside to the wall.

Mandy raced to catch up with her. "Wait, Your Highness! I need to ask you something!"

Mandy wanted to show Cleopatra the Hero's Collar and find out who owned it. She struggled to unwrap the cat. But Cleopatra had already reached the wall and boosted herself halfway up.

"There she is! The imposter!" several gruff voices shouted from the other side. "Arrest her."

Jake and Mandy expected to see Cleopatra jump back down and run away. Instead, she stood on top of the wall and faced the guards with her hands on her hips. Her voice rang out strongly in the night air.

"Seth, if you come one step closer, I will see to it that you, your children, and your children's children will never step foot in Egypt again!"

The head of the palace guards froze when he heard Cleopatra call him by name. He gestured to the other soldiers making their way along the wall to stop. "Princess?" he asked. "Is it really you?"

Cleopatra slowly turned to look at all the people standing in the palace garden. "I am Cleopatra, the Sun God's daughter. Who dares to question me?"

"I do," a deep voice replied.

Instantly Cleopatra dropped to one knee. All those around her knelt even lower, pressing their foreheads against the ground.

Jake and Mandy huddled together on the other side of the wall with the cat.

"I guess we know who that is," Mandy whispered in her quietest voice.

Jake nodded. "Big Daddy Pharoah!"

Chapter Eleven
Cleopatra's Father

Cleopatra stayed down on one knee and did not even dare to raise her head. The guards stayed face down on the wall. Mandy and Jake held their breaths, waiting for lightning to strike.

Finally Cleopatra broke the silence. "I am your daughter, oh Great One," she said, keeping her head bowed. "Why would you think otherwise?"

"The Prince of Persia and your own brother have called you an imposter," her father replied.

"The prince, I'm sure, is a wise man, but he could be mistaken," Cleopatra replied. "He has never met me until today. My brother, on the other hand, has called me many names. I'm not surprised that Tolly would add 'imposter' to the list."

Cleopatra's use of her brother's nickname sent a murmur around the garden. Cleopatra heard the murmur and smiled down at Mandy and Jake, who were only a few feet below her, huddled against the wall.

The Pharaoh cleared his throat and said, "You are not dressed like my daughter. My daughter would never appear in unwashed rags like a peasant."

"Oh, no," Mandy whispered. "Now she's going to have to tell about switching places, and she'll make me appear."

But Cleopatra's response took her by surprise.

"A future queen of Egypt is not defined by her clothes, my father," Cleopatra answered. "In my private garden, I may dress as I wish."

Jake peeked above the wall to see how the Pharaoh would react to Cleopatra's words. The

Pharaoh was consulting his advisor, Ash. Then Ash nodded and stepped forward. "There is one test that will prove that you are who you say you are," he declared.

Cleopatra lifted her head for the first time and looked her father directly in the eye. "Test me."

"I gave to you a gift earlier today," the Pharaoh said. "You were supposed to present it to the Prince of Persia." His eyes narrowed. "Where is that gift?"

Cleopatra didn't answer.

Ash stepped forward. "The Great One has asked you a question," he shouted. "You must answer it."

Cleopatra shifted uncomfortably on the wall. Finally she muttered, "I, um, lost it."

Someone burst out laughing from behind the Pharaoh. It was Cleopatra's brother. He stepped forward and said, "That's a likely story. You don't even know what it is." He looked up at his father. "She's an imposter, like I told you."

"I am not an imposter, you worm!" Cleopatra shouted at her brother. "I know what he gave me.

It was a golden Hero's Collar."

Jake gasped, "The Hero's Collar is Cleopatra's. Mandy! Give it to her and let's go home!"

Mandy groaned, "I can't. If I give her the Hero's Collar, she'll have to marry the Prince of Persia."

"So?" Jake hissed.

"If she marries the Prince of Persia, she can't become the Queen of Egypt," Mandy explained. "And she has to. That's history, and we don't want to change it."

"You *lost* the Hero's Collar?" the Pharaoh's angry voice boomed from the other side of the wall.

Cleopatra's voice dropped as she explained, "I put it on my cat to see how it looked, and then she disappeared."

"You see? This is Cleopatra's cat!" Jake punched Mandy in the arm. "Now give her the collar, or we'll be stuck here forever."

Mandy shook her head stubbornly. "We can't until we solve the Prince of Persia problem."

Cleopatra looked very nervous standing on the wall above them. Her brother had called her an imposter. Her father was angry with her. She whispered, "Isis! Help!"

Cleopatra's words were like magic and Mandy sprang into action. She was still wearing Cleopatra's jewels and dress. She handed Jake the cat and leaped onto the wall next to Cleopatra. Everyone in the courtyard gasped.

"Hear me, people of Egypt!" Mandy boomed. "I am a messenger from the goddess Isis."

Mandy quickly surveyed the scene. The garden was filled with guards with torches, servants, guests from the banquet—all of them kneeling before Mandy. Even the great Ash, Cleopatra's brother, and the Prince of Persia were on their knees.

All of them but the Pharaoh. He looked just like the pictures Mandy had seen in books. He wore a white skirt, a gold collar around his neck, and a red and gold striped headdress. He stood alone, his arms crossed, a fierce look on his face. Even from the wall she could feel his power. Mandy would have lost her nerve to go on if Jake hadn't pinched the back of her foot.

"Hear the will of Isis!" Mandy squeaked. "Cleopatra shall not marry the Prince of Persia."

The crowd gasped. The Prince of Persia looked very disappointed but said nothing.

"A greater destiny awaits her," Mandy continued. "She is to be the Queen of the Nile."

"What?" Cleopatra's brother yelped.

"Silence!" Mandy shouted at the boy. "And to prove that Isis means business—" Mandy gestured for Jake to hand her the collar, but Jake was having trouble getting it off the cat.

"Give me the collar!" she said between clenched teeth. "And let's get out of here!"

Jake was sweating. "I can't unhook it. It's stuck," he called from behind the wall.

The people in the garden were starting to get restless. They wondered who Mandy was speaking to.

Frustrated, Mandy threw her arms in the air and shouted, "Then just give me the cat. But give me something!"

Jake leaped onto the wall and lost his balance. Mandy grabbed his arm, but she was

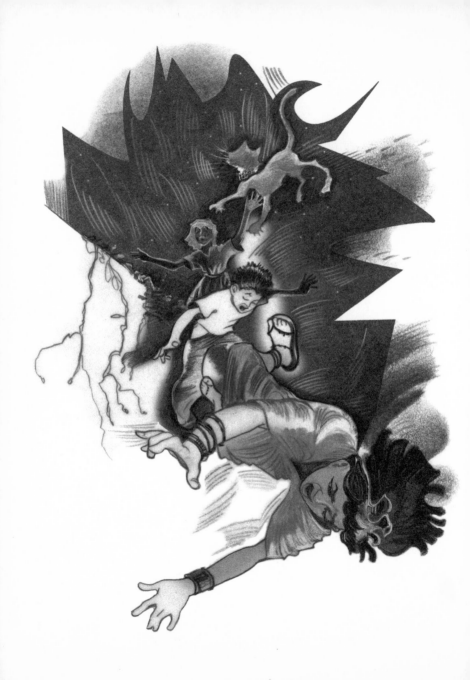

thrown off balance, too. As they fell backwards, Mandy tossed the cat, which was still wearing the Hero's Collar, into Cleopatra's arms. "Good-bye, Cleo, and good luck!"

The moment Cleopatra caught the cat, Mandy and Jake vanished into thin air.

Chapter Twelve
Home Again

The trip back to the Strange Museum took much longer than it ever had before. But then again (as Jake pointed out later), they did have a lot more time to cover—more than 2,000 years. When the lights stopped flashing and the room stopped spinning, they took a second to get their bearings.

"They were no longer dressed in their Egyptian outfits. They were back in their jeans and T-shirts. As usual, their world looked the same except for a slight change.

"Look." Jake pointed to the display case. "The glass isn't broken, but the Hero's Collar is gone, and something else has taken its place."

Mandy took a step forward and peered into the glass case. There on the velvet pedestal was a gold crown in the shape of a cobra snake. Just minutes before, it had been on her own head.

Mandy spun in a circle. Something was missing. "The cat didn't make it back," she said. "I don't see him anywhere." Her voice was hollow with disappointment.

Jake was disappointed, too. "It was Cleopatra's cat. I guess we should be happy that he found his way home."

"Right," Mandy said. Usually their trips back in time had left them feeling excited. Now she just felt sad.

"Come on," Jake said, patting her on the shoulder. "Let's go upstairs. It's almost dinner time."

Mandy took one last look at the room, hoping she might see a little pink nose or a pair of ears peek out from behind one of the display cases. But the room was definitely empty. She flicked off the light and followed her brother up to the third floor.

When they reached their home on the third floor, their father was standing in the doorway.

"Greetings, children!" Dr. Strange said in an extra cheery voice. "You're just in time to see the latest addition to our museum."

Normally Mandy and Jake liked to see the new pieces that came into the museum. Tonight they just didn't feel like it.

Dr. Strange waved them into the living room. "Come inside, I don't want it to run away."

Jake raised an eyebrow at Mandy. "Run away?" he repeated. Jake didn't know of one museum piece that could run away.

Dr. Strange laughed and shook his head. "I was just kidding."

"I thought so," Jake replied.

"It's too tiny to run away," their father added.

Mandy put her hands on her hips and said, "All right. I give up. What are you talking about?"

"Shhhhh!" Dr. Strange warned. "You might wake her."

"Her?" Jake and Mandy repeated.

They watched as their father carefully reached into the pocket of his jacket and pulled out a tiny ball of gray fur.

"It's a kitten!" Mandy cried with glee.

"It's very strange," their father explained as he placed the tiny little furball in the palm of Mandy's hand. "We were unpacking the new shipment for our Egyptian collection, when this kitten just appeared."

Mandy and Jake exchanged looks but said nothing.

"Has Mom seen her?" Jake asked as he reached out to stroke the top of the little kitten's head.

"Your mother's the one who found her," Dr. Strange said.

"Can we keep her?" Mandy asked. She squeezed her eyes closed, waiting for her father to say no. What he said next took her completely by surprise.

"We have to keep her," their father replied, smiling down at the little kitten. "She's too tiny to be left on her own."

Mandy and Jake looked at each other. "But what about Mom?" Jake asked. "Won't she worry that the cat might be a problem in the museum?"

Their father waved one hand. "Your mother is really an old softie. We discussed it, and she said a cat is just fine as long as it stays up here in our home on the third floor."

"All right!" Jake cried with glee.

"Hurray!" Mandy cried as she held the kitten up in the air to look at its little face.

"We've really only got one problem," their father added.

"What's that?" Jake asked.

"What should we call her?" Dr. Strange asked. "She needs a name."

The tiny little kitten blinked her jade green eyes at Jake and Mandy, and they grinned at each other. They knew instantly what her name would be.

"Cleo."

About the Authors

JAHNNA N. MALCOLM stands for Jahnna "and" Malcolm. Jahnna Beecham and Malcolm Hillgartner are married and have published over ninety books for kids and teens. They've written about ballerinas, horses, ghosts, singing cowboys, and green slime. Their most recent book series is called The Jewel Kingdom, and it is about adventurous princesses. They even made a movie of the first book in the series, *The Ruby Princess Runs Away*.

Before Jahnna and Malcolm wrote books, they were actors. They met on the stage and were married on the stage, and now they live in Oregon. They used to think of their ideas for their books by themselves. Now they get help from their son, Dash, and daughter, Skye.

About the Illustrator

SALLY WERN COMPORT'S illustrations have been seen nationally for over fifteen years. A 1976 graduate of Columbus College of Art & Design, she began her career as an art director at several agencies before beginning full-time illustration in 1983. Her work has received numerous honors including The Society of Illustrators, Communication Arts, *Print* magazine, *How* magazine, and many Addy awards.

Sally's artwork has been included in several permanent collections, including Women Illustrators from the permanent collection of The Society of Illustrators. Her first children's book, *Brave Margaret*, was released in February 1999. Sally lives with her husband and two children in Annapolis, Maryland.

While the events, locations, and characters described in this book may be based on actual historical events and real people, this story is fictional.